rhcbooks.com

ISBN 978-0-7364-4274-9 (trade) — ISBN 978-0-7364-4275-6 (ebook)

Printed in the United States of America
10 9 8 7 6 5 4 3 2 1

TURNING RED

THE GRAPHIC NOVEL

Random House 🏠 New York

FAMILY MATTERS

MEILIN LEE (MEI)

Academic all-star Meilin is rocking eighth grade: scoring straight As, excelling in band, and making plans with her besties to change the world. She's a star in her mom's eyes, too—the perfect obedient daughter who does her chores like clockwork and is always eager to please. In fact, Meilin's number-one rule is "Honor your parents." She makes it all look easy . . . until she discovers the ancient magic behind her family's really big secret. Keeping it all together is a lot harder when you're charged up with hormones—and covered with red fur!

RED PANDA MEI

Middle school is challenging enough, but imagine navigating that social minefield knowing that one laugh, cry, or burst of anger can transform you into a giant red panda! When Meilin gets emotional, she poofs into an eight-foot-tall hormone-fueled red panda with an adorable but highly destructive fluffy tail.

FAMILY MATTERS

MING LEE

Meilin's elegant and fierce mom is always in control . . . of herself and everything else! Ming is the devoted keeper of the Lee family Temple, and for years Melini has rushed home from school to help her mother clean and maintain the temple and entertain its guests. Perfectionist Ming expects the best from her precious daughter, and Meilin does everything she can to make her mom happy. No matter what, Ming has a deep love for her family.

JIN LEE

Quiet, thoughtful Jin brings a calming balance to his wife Ming's strong-willed nature. He loves to cook for his family, enjoys gardening, and adores his daughter, Meilin. When adolescent angst causes storms between his daughter and his wife, Jin does his best to help hold the family steady.

FRIENDSHIP FOREVER!

MIRIAM MENDELSOHN

One of Meilin's besties, thirteen-year-old Miriam is everything a best friend should be—loyal, funny, and supportive. She's always there to coax Meilin into an impromptu dance party or lend her a prized 4*Town CD. And she is one hundred percent there for Meilin's growing independence from her mom.

PRIYA MANGAL

Priya might be the most subdued of Meilin's crew, but her friends know she's a bit of a wild card with a deadpan sense of humor. She's quick to jump to Meilin's defense, especially against that gigantic dork Tyler. And like the rest of Meilin's crew, Priya's obsessed with the boy band 4*Town.

FRIENDSHIP FOREVER!

ABBY PARK

Abby is a big friend in a small package—tiny but fiercely protective of her besties and ready for any adventure. She's fired up about everything, from her projects to protect the environment to her choice for cutest boy band: 4*Town, obviously! And her fists of fury are ready to whale on anyone who messes with her friends.

TYLER NGUYEN-BAKER

Meilin's archnemesis, Tyler, has the annoying habit of popping up just in time to make an embarrassing situation even worse. He makes fun of others and cracks jokes at their expense, never missing a chance to kick someone when they're down. Tyler's jerkish, aggressive behavior is really an attempt to protect himself from being labeled a loser, but it doesn't win him many friends.

4*TOWN FOREVER!

4*TOWN

In 2002, the biggest boy band in the world is 4*Town (which, strangely, has five members). Robaire, Tae Young, Jesse, Aaron Z, and Aaron T are not only great singers and hype dancers, but they also write their own songs. No wonder Meilin and her besties each dream of marrying a different band member. They'll do whatever they have to do—including launching Operation: 4*Town Shakedown— to get tickets to the 4*Town concert.

FAMILY REUNION

GRANDMA

Ming's demanding, critical mother sets high expectations for her daughter and granddaughter. Fortunately for the Lee family, Grandma turned over the family temple to Ming years ago and is now content to critique her life from afar. But when she suspects Ming has let Meilin's red panda situation get out of hand, Grandma is at their doorstep in a heartbeat, sisters and cousins in tow, to take charge.

THE AUNTIES AND COUSINS

Both Meilin and Ming are surprised when Grandma shows up, along with Ming's glamorous aunts and cousins. Grandma's younger sisters, Auntie Chen and Auntie Ping, bring their own daughters, Cousin Helen and Cousin Lily. Auntie Chen is petite and bossy. Her daughter, Helen, can be grumpy, but she loves her family. Auntie Ping is a legendary cook, and her daughter, Lily, is a drama queen.

AS YOU KNOW, OUR ANCESTOR SUN YEE HAD A MYSTICAL CONNECTION WITH RED PANDAS.

IN FACT, SHE LOVED THEM SO MUCH...

...THAT SHE ASKED THE GODS TO TURN HER INTO ONE.

IT WAS WARTIME. THE MEN WERE ALL GONE.

SUN YEE WAS DESPERATE FOR A WAY TO PROTECT HERSELF AND HER DAUGHTERS.

THEN ONE NIGHT, DURING A RED MOON, THE GODS GRANTED HER WISH.

THEY GAVE HER THE ABILITY TO HARNESS HER EMOTIONS TO TRANSFORM INTO A POWERFUL, MYSTICAL BEAST.

SUN YEE PASSED THIS GIFT TO HER DAUGHTERS FOR WHEN THEY CAME OF AGE. AND THEY PASSED IT TO THEIRS... BUT OVER TIME, OUR FAMILY CHOSE TO COME TO A NEW WORLD.

AND WHAT WAS A BLESSING BECAME... AN INCONVENIENCE.

ARE YOU SERIOUS?!

SHE MEANT IT AS A BLESSING!

IT'S A CURSE! YOU CURSED US! IT'S ALL YOUR FAULT!

WHY DIDN'T YOU WARN ME?

I THOUGHT I HAD MORE TIME! IF I WATCHED YOU LIKE A HAWK, I'D SEE THE SIGNS, BE ABLE TO PREPARE!

BUT IT'S GOING TO BE FINE. I OVERCAME IT, AND YOU WILL TOO.

"ON THE NEXT RED MOON, YOU'LL UNDERGO A RITUAL THAT WILL SEAL YOUR RED PANDA SPIRIT INTO A PENDANT. AND THEN YOU WILL BE CURED FOR GOOD. JUST LIKE ME."

POOF

"BUT ANY STRONG EMOTION WILL RELEASE THE PANDA. AND THE MORE YOU RELEASE IT, THE MORE DIFFICULT THE RITUAL WILL BE."

PLEASE... JUST... GO AWAY!

"THERE IS A DARKNESS TO THE PANDA, MEI-MEI. YOU HAVE ONLY ONE CHANCE TO BANISH IT, AND YOU CANNOT FAIL. OTHERWISE, YOU'LL NEVER BE FREE."

TAP TAP TAP

MEI, IT'S US! OPEN UP!

"THE NEXT RED MOON IS JUST ONE MONTH AWAY, ON THE 25TH."

WE WERE SO WORRIED!

WE THOUGHT YOU DIED OF EMBARRASSMENT!

ARE YOU OKAY? TAP IF YOU CAN HEAR US!

GUYS, WHAT ARE YOU DOING? GO AWAY!

FORGET THAT! 4*TOWN IS COMING TO TORONTO! MAY 18TH!

LATER...

READY.

DEFORESTATION.

...

SAD ORANGUTAN.

NGHHHH...

YOUR SECOND-PLACE SPELLING TROPHY.

WHAT... A... SHAME.

HOW... ADORABLE.

HOW IS THIS POSSIBLE?! WHAT HAPPENED TO YOUR PANDA?!

WHEN I START TO GET EMOTIONAL, I IMAGINE THE PEOPLE I LOVE MOST... WHICH IS... YOU GUYS.

SO NOW THAT'S SETTLED, I JUST HAVE ONE TEENY TINY FAVOR TO ASK...

A FEW MINUTES LATER...

NO! ABSOLUTELY NOT! IT'S ONE THING TO STAY CALM AT HOME, BUT A CONCERT? YOU'LL PANDA ALL OVER THE PLACE!

WHAT? BUT THIS IS ONCE IN A LIFETIME!

4*TOWN WHY I MUST GO

MAYBE WE SHOULD TRUST HER.

IT'S THEM I DON'T TRUST! LOOK AT THOSE GLITTERY DELINQUENTS WITH THEIR, UGH, GYRATIONS!

NO CONCERT, AND THAT'S FINAL.

AM I THE ONLY ONE WHO SEES THE DANGER HERE? THERE'S NO WAY SHE COULD KEEP HER PANDA IN!

BRRRING

IT'S YOUR MOTHER.

MING, I KNOW ABOUT MEI-MEI.

I WAS JUST ABOUT TO CALL YOU. BUT EVERYTHING'S FINE. I'M GOING TO HANDLE THE RITUAL ON MY OWN—

THE WAY YOU HANDLED MEI-MEI BEING ON THE NEWS?

I'M ON MY WAY. WITH REINFORCEMENTS.

LATER, THAT EVENING...

OKAY, I'M OFF TO MATHLETES!

WAIT! I MADE ALL YOUR FAVORITES!

THANKS, BUT... MIRIAM'S DAD IS ORDERING PIZZA. SAVE ME LEFTOVERS?

WHAT IF I CAME WITH YOU? I WAS MATHLETES CHAMP IN GRADE EIGHT, YOU KNOW.

COOL... OH, *JADE PALACE* IS ON TONIGHT. CAN'T MISS THAT, RIGHT?

NOW, WHO'S THE WEAK LINK? PRIYA AND ABBY SEEM BRIGHT ENOUGH, BUT MIRIAM...

AND TRAFFIC'S A NIGHTMARE!

I MEAN, SHE'S A NICE GIRL, BUT MAYBE SHE'S SLOWING YOU DOWN...

MOM, I DON'T WANT YOU TO COME!

RUMBLE

HEY, DAD. I'M ALMOST READY.

WHAT HAS YOUR MOTHER TOLD YOU ABOUT HER PANDA?

NOTHING. SHE WON'T TALK ABOUT IT.

IT WAS QUITE DESTRUCTIVE. SHE ALMOST TOOK OUT HALF THE TEMPLE.

YOU SAW IT?

ONLY ONCE. SHE AND YOUR GRANDMA HAD A TERRIBLE FIGHT.

OVER WHAT?

YOUR GRANDMA DID NOT APPROVE OF ME. BUT YOU SHOULD HAVE SEEN YOUR MOM. SHE WAS... INCREDIBLE.

PEOPLE HAVE ALL KINDS OF SIDES TO THEM. AND SOME SIDES ARE... MESSY.

THE POINT IS NOT TO PUSH THE BAD STUFF AWAY. IT'S TO MAKE ROOM FOR IT, LIVE WITH IT.

MEI-MEI, IT'S TIME.

ONE MONTH LATER...

"I'M MEILIN LEE, AND EVER SINCE I TURNED THIRTEEN, LIFE'S BEEN... A LOT. MOM AND I JUST CALL IT... GROWING PAINS."

"THINGS AT THE TEMPLE HAVE NEVER BEEN BETTER."

YOU READY?

LET'S DO THIS.

HELLO! WELCOME TO OUR TEMPLE!

WHAT UP, TORONTO! GET IN HERE!

OUR TEMPLE IS THE OLDEST IN TORONTO AND THE ONLY ONE THAT'S HOME TO THE GREAT RED PANDA!

SAY "BAMBOO LEAVES!"

BAMBOO LEAVES!

MEI!

YO. WHAT UP?

HEY, FURBALL.

READY TO GET YOUR KARAOKE ON?

TOTALLY!

POOF

BYE, MOM. BYE, DAD. I'LL BE BACK BEFORE DINNER, 'KAY?

FINE.

OH, UM— YOU'RE WELCOME TO JOIN US.

FOR MR. LEE'S COOKING?

DUDE, YES.

MMMM!

WE ARE SO THERE.

"AND YEAH, SOMETIMES I MISS HOW THINGS WERE, BUT... NOTHING STAYS THE SAME FOREVER."

"WE'VE ALL GOT AN INNER BEAST. WE'VE ALL GOT A MESSY, LOUD... WEIRD PART OF OURSELVES HIDDEN AWAY. AND A LOT OF US NEVER LET IT OUT."

"BUT I DID. HOW ABOUT YOU?"

THE END

"I'M A FURRY TICKING TIME BOMB!"

–MEILIN

"I'M CHANGING, MOM. I'M FINALLY FIGURING OUT WHO I AM. BUT I'M SCARED IT'LL TAKE ME AWAY FROM YOU."

—MEILIN

GRAPHIC NOVEL

SCRIPT ADAPTATION
Amy Chu

LAYOUT
Emilio Urbano

INK
Marco Forcelloni,
Andrea Greppi

COLOR
Massimo Rocca,
Angela Capolupo-Maaw Art Team,
Maria Claudia Di Genova

LETTERS
Chris Dickey

COVER

LAYOUT
Emilio Urbano

INK
Marco Forcelloni

COLOR
Maria Claudia Di Genova

DISNEY PUBLISHING WORLDWIDE
Global Magazines, Comics, and Partworks

PUBLISHER
Lynn Waggoner

EXECUTIVE EDITOR
Carlotta Quattrocolo

EDITORIAL TEAM
Bianca Coletti (Director, Magazines), Guido
Frazzini (Director, Comics), Stefano Ambrosio
(Executive Editor), Camilla Vedove (Senior Man-
ager, Editorial Development), Behnoosh Khalili
(Senior Editor), Julie Dorris (Senior Editor),
Mina Riazi (Assistant Editor), Gabriela Capasso
(Assistant Editor)

DESIGN
Enrico Soave (Senior Designer)

ART
Ken Shue (VP, Global Art),
Roberto Santillo (Creative Director),
Manny Mederos (Senior Illustration
Manager),
Marco Ghiglione (Creative Manager),
Stefano Attardi (Illustration Manager)

PORTFOLIO MANAGEMENT
Olivia Ciancarelli (Director)

BUSINESS & MARKETING
Mariantonietta Galla
(Senior Manager, Franchise)
Virpi Korhonen (Editorial Manager)

GRAPHIC DESIGN
Chris Dickey

EDITORIAL WRITING
Deb Barnes

CONTRIBUTOR
Simona Grandi

SPECIAL THANKS
Scott Tilley, Nick Balian